For my parents

First U.S. small hardcover edition 2002

The Library of Congress has cataloged the large hardcover second edition as follows:

Handford, Martin.
[Find Waldo now!]
Where's Waldo now? / Martin Handford. — 2nd U.S. ed.
p.   cm.
Summary: The reader follows Waldo as he travels through different time periods in history
and must try to find him in the illustrations of some of the crowded events in which he participates.
ISBN 0-7636-0308-2 (large hardcover)
[1.Time travel—Fiction. 2. Humorous stories. 3. Picture puzzles.] I. Title.
PZ7.H1918Whg   1997
[Fic]—dc21   97-013734
ISBN 0-7636-1921-3 (small hardcover)

2 4 6 8 10 9 7 5 3 1

Printed in Hong Kong

This book was typeset in Optima.
The illustrations were done in watercolor and water-based ink.

Candlewick Press
2067 Massachusetts Avenue
Cambridge, Massachusetts 02140

visit us at www.candlewick.com

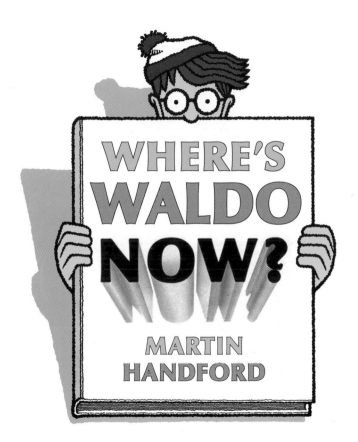

WHERE'S WALDO NOW?

MARTIN HANDFORD

CANDLEWICK PRESS
CAMBRIDGE, MASSACHUSETTS

HI THERE, BOOKWORMS!

SOME PARTS OF HISTORY ARE AMAZING!
I SIT HERE READING ALL THESE BOOKS
ABOUT THE WORLD LONG AGO, AND IT'S
LIKE RIDING A TIME MACHINE. WHY NOT
TRY IT FOR YOURSELVES? JUST SEARCH
EACH PICTURE AND FIND ME, WOOF
(REMEMBER, ALL YOU CAN SEE IS HIS TAIL),
WENDA, WIZARD WHITEBEARD, AND ODLAW.
THEN LOOK FOR MY KEY, WOOF'S BONE
(IN THIS SCENE IT'S THE BONE THAT'S
NEAREST TO HIS TAIL), WENDA'S CAMERA,
WIZARD WHITEBEARD'S SCROLL, AND
ODLAW'S BINOCULARS.

THERE ARE ALSO 25 WALDO-WATCHERS,
EACH OF WHOM APPEARS ONLY ONCE
SOMEWHERE ON MY TRAVELS. AND ONE
MORE THING! CAN YOU FIND ANOTHER
CHARACTER, NOT SHOWN BELOW, WHO
APPEARS ONCE IN EVERY PICTURE?

Waldo

4,578 YEARS AGO

THE RIDDLE OF THE PYRAMIDS

The Ancient Egyptians were very clever people who loved goats, cats, and sphinx, and invented pyramids. They built several huge pyramids in the desert. But now no one can remember why. Were they adventure playgrounds for Egyptian mommies and babies, or were they houses without doors or windows?

To answer those questions and to find me can be as hard as a camel's hump.

2,000 YEARS AGO

FUN AND GAMES IN ANCIENT ROME

The Romans spent most of their time fighting, conquering, learning Latin, and making roads. They always had games at the Coliseum. Their favorite games were fighting, chariot racing, fighting, and feeding Christians to the lions. When the crowd gave a gladiator the thumbs down, it meant kill your opponent. Thumbs up meant let him go. Thumbs up for you if you can find me at the games.

1,003 YEARS AGO

ON TOUR WITH THE VIKINGS

At home, the Vikings were quiet people who liked knitting and cheese tasting and boring things like that. But on tour, they went wild. They put on their best horned hats and sailed across the sea, singing and shouting like mad. If you heard them coming, it was best to run away. But don't you run away before you find me.

800 YEARS AGO

THE END OF THE CRUSADES

After 200 years of fierce argument with the Saladins and Paladins, who would not tell them the way to Jerusalem, the Crusaders finally ran out of clean T-shirts, so they came home. For years afterward they dined out on stories of the castles they had battered and besieged and the fascinating people they had thrown rocks at. Go on your own crusade to find me.

ONCE UPON A SATURDAY MORNING

The Middle Ages were a very merry time to be alive, especially on Saturdays. Short skirts and striped tights were in fashion for men; everybody knew lots of jokes; and there was widespread juggling, jousting, archery, jesting, and fun. But if you got into trouble, the Middle Ages could be miserable. For the man in the stocks or the pillory or about to lose his head, Saturday morning was no laughing matter. Don't joke around, look for me here.

THE LAST DAYS OF THE AZTECS

The Aztecs lived in sunny Mexico and were rich and strong and liked swinging from poles pretending to be eagles. They also liked making human sacrifices to their gods, so it was best to agree with everything they said. The Spanish were also rich and strong and some of them, called conquistadores, came to Mexico to find gold. They thought the Aztecs a complete nuisance. Get swinging and find me in Mexico.

400 YEARS AGO

Is red better than blue? What do you mean your poem about cherry blossoms is better than mine? Shall we have another cup of tea? Over difficult questions such as these, the Japanese fought fiercely for hundreds of years. The fiercest fighters of all were the samurai, who wore flags on their backs so that their mommies could find them. The fighters without flags were called ashigaru. I don't have a flag either, but find me anyway.

TROUBLE IN OLD JAPAN

BEING A PIRATE

(Shiver-me-timbers!)

It really was a lot of fun being a pirate, especially if you were very hairy and didn't have much in the way of brains. It also helped if you had only one leg, or one eye, or two noses, and had a pirate's hat with your name tag sewn inside and a treasure map and a rusty cutlass. Once there were lots of pirates, but they died out in the end because too many of them were men. Shiver-me-timbers and find me here.

HAVING A BALL
IN
GAYE PAREE

The history of France has some very bad parts, like getting your head chopped off by Madame Guillotine in the French Revolution; and some very good parts, like the invention of smelly cheese. In 1870 Napoleon (the third one) threw a ball in Paris to celebrate. All the beautiful people came and danced the night away to a band called the Third Republic. Waltz right in and find me.

THE GOLD RUSH

At the end of the nineteenth century large numbers of Americans were frequently seen to be rushing toward holes in the ground, hoping to find gold. Most of them never even found the holes in the ground. But at least they all got exercise and fresh air, which kept them healthy. And health is more important than gold . . . isn't it? You get the gold if you can spot me.

WALDO IS LOST
IN THE FUTURE!
FIND HIM! RESCUE HIM!
WALDO'S BOOKS ARE LOST
IN THE PAST!
FIND THEM! RESCUE THEM!
THERE'S ONE LOST IN EACH
PICTURE. GO BACK
AND LOOK FOR THEM!
WHERE'S WALDO?
FIND WALDO NOW.

THE GREAT WHERE'S WALDO NOW? CHECKLIST
Hundreds more things for time travelers to look for!

THE STONE AGE
- Four cavemen swinging into trouble
- An accident with an axe
- A great invention
- A Stone-Age rodeo
- Boars chasing a man
- Men chasing a boar
- A romantic caveman
- A mammoth squirt
- A man who has overeaten
- A bear trap
- A mammoth in the river
- A fruit stall
- Charging woolly rhinos
- A big cover-up
- A trunk holding a trunk
- A knockout game of baseball
- A rocky picture show
- An upside-down boar
- A spoilt dog
- A lesson on dinosaurs
- A very scruffy family
- Some dangerous spear fishermen

THE RIDDLE OF THE PYRAMIDS
- An upside-down pyramid
- An upside-down sarcophagus
- A group of posing gods
- Two protruding hands
- Two protruding feet
- A fat man and his picture
- Seventeen protruding tongues
- Stones defying gravity
- Egyptian graffiti
- Egyptian vandals
- A man sweeping dirt under a pyramid
- A thirsty sphinx
- A runaway block of stone
- A loud blast
- A happy leopard
- A picture firing an arrow
- A careless water-carrier
- Sunbathers in peril
- A messy milking session
- A mummy and a baby
- Pyramids of sand

FUN AND GAMES IN ANCIENT ROME
- A charioteer who has lost his chariot
- Coliseum cleaners
- An unequal contest with spears
- A winner who is about to lose
- A lion with good table manners
- A deadly set of wheels
- Lion cubs being teased
- Four shields that match their owners
- A pyramid of lions
- Lions giving the paws down
- A leopard chasing a leopard skin
- A piggyback puncher
- An awful musician
- A painful fork-lift
- A horse holding the reins
- A leopard in love
- A Roman keeping count
- A gladiator losing his sandals

ON TOUR WITH THE VIKINGS
- A happy figurehead
- Figureheads in love
- A man being used as a club
- A tearful sheep
- Two hopeless hiding places
- Childish Vikings
- A beard with a foot on it
- An eagle posing as a helmet
- A sailor tearing a sail
- A heavily armed Viking
- A ride on a braid
- Three spears being beheaded
- A burning behind
- A bent boat
- A frightened figurehead
- Locked horns
- A helmet with spiders
- A helmet of smoke
- A bullfight

THE END OF THE CRUSADES
- A cat about to be catapulted
- A man about to be catapulted
- A human bridge
- A key that's out of reach
- A message for the milkman
- A cauldron of boiling oil
- A battering-ram
- Crusaders caught by their necks
- A load of washing
- Two catapult catastrophes
- A catapult aiming the wrong way
- Three snakes
- A crusader fast asleep
- Crusaders soaking up the sun
- Flattened crusaders
- Rockfaces
- A crusader who broke a ladder
- A ticklish situation

ONCE UPON A SATURDAY MORNING
- A dirty downpour
- Archers missing the target
- A jouster sitting back to front
- A dog stalking a cat stalking some birds
- A long line of pickpockets
- A jouster who needs lots of practice
- A man making a bear dance
- A bear making a man dance
- Hats that are tied together
- Fruit and vegetable thieves
- An unexpected puddle
- A juggling jester
- A very long drink
- A heavily burdened beast
- Drunken friars
- A man scything hats
- An angry fish
- A ticklish torture
- Minstrels making an awful noise